# Moss and Blister

## Garfield's Apprentices

*Already published*

1. The Lamplighter's Funeral
2. Mirror, Mirror
3. Moss and Blister

*In preparation*

5. The Valentine
6. Labour in Vain
7. The Fool
8. Rosy Starling
9. The Dumb Cake
10. Tom Titmarsh's Devil
11. The Filthy Beast
12. The Enemy

# LEON GARFIELD

*Illustrated by*
FAITH JAQUES

HEINEMANN
*London*

William Heinemann Ltd
15 Queen Street, Mayfair, London W1X 8BE

LONDON MELBOURNE TORONTO
JOHANNESBURG AUCKLAND

To Vivien

First published 1976


434 94033 x

Printed and bound in Great Britain by
Morrison & Gibb Ltd., London and Edinburgh

There they go, Moss and Blister, hurrying up Blackfriar's Stairs and on through the dark streets, under a sky fairly peppered with stars as cold as frozen sparks. Up Coalman's Alley, across Bristol Street . . .

"'appy Christmas, marm—and a nappy Christmas to you, miss!" bellowed a bellman, coming out of an ale-house and wagging his bell like a swollen brass finger.

"*For unto us a Child is born, unto us a Son is given!*" he hiccupped; and read out a little Christmas poem of his own composing while Moss and Blister stood stock still and listened. Then he held out his hand and Moss put a sixpence in it, for it was Christmas Eve, and Moss, who was a midwife, felt holy and important.

Ordinarily Moss was brisk and businesslike to a degree; but on this one night of the year she was as soft as butter and gave her services for nothing. She lived in hopes of being summoned to a stable and delivering the Son of God.

"It's written down, Blister," she said to her apprentice, after the bellman had weaved away. "It's all written down. *Unto them that look for him shall he appear the second time.*"

Blister, a tall, thin girl with sticking-out ears and saucer eyes, who flapped and stalked after stubby Moss like a loose umbrella, said: "Yus'm!" and looked frightened to death. Blister also had her dream of Christmas Eve and a stable; but it was not quite the same as Moss's. She dreamed that Moss would be delivering *her* of the marvellous Child.

Naturally she kept her ambition a deep secret from Moss, so that the dreamy frown that sometimes settled on her face led Moss to surmise that her apprentice was a deep one . . . Mostly these frowns came in the springtime, for Moss knew it would take nine months . . . which was one less than the toes on both her feet. At the end of every March she'd lie in her bed, waiting with ghostly urgency for Moss to appear beside her; for Moss had a gift like the angel of the annunciation. She could tell, long before it showed, if any female had a bun in the oven, a cargo in the hold or a deposit in the vault—depending on the trade concerned.

She'd stop dead in the street, fix her eye in a certain way upon some lightsome lass, dig Blister in the ribs, and follow the female to her home. Then she'd leave her card and everyone in the neighbourhood would know that a happy event was on the way. Truly, the sight of Moss, in her ancient cape that was green with rain and age, was as sure a sign of pregnancy as morning sickness or a passion for pickles.

But she never looked at Blister in that certain way; and every Christmas Eve Blister would grow frightened that someone else had been chosen to bear the glory of the world. The dreamy frown, but now tinged with apprehension and melancholy, settled on her face as she floundered on in Moss's wake.

"Make 'aste, marm!" shrieked out a link-boy, streaking his torch along a row of railings so that a fringe of fire fell down and iron shadows marched across the houses like the army of the Lord. "Cat's 'avin' kittens!"

"There's a imp for impidence!" puffed Moss, shaking her fist and making as if to rush upon the hastily fleeing offender. "Just let me catch 'im and I'll pop 'im back where 'e came from!"

"Just let *me* catch 'im!" screeched Blister, shaking her fist likewise, so that midwife and apprentice made a pattern in the street of wrath in two sizes.

Then Moss gave up and beckoned to Blister; there was no time to waste; they were needed in Glass House Yard where Mrs Greening's waters had broken and the whole household was having contractions in sympathy.

"D'yer fink it'll be the one?" panted Blister, swinging her heavy business bag from one hand to the other. "You know. '*im* what's comin' for the second time?" Her voice trembled, and so did her lip.

"Nar," said Moss. "It's got to be in a stable, Blister. Ain't I told you that? There's got to be a donkey and three kings and wise men with frankincense and—and more."

"Wot's frankincense?"

"It's a sort of fruit. Summat between a orringe and a pommygrunt," answered Moss, who did not care to appear ill-informed.

Blister nodded. They really were pig-ignorant, the pair

of them; although why a pig, who knows where to find truffles and live the good life, should be put on a level with Moss and Blister, passes understanding. Moss didn't even know that the world was round, while Blister didn't know that China was a place as well as a cup. Moss's arithmetic —apart from counting out her fee, about which she was remarkably sharp—was confined to the natural proposition that one and one, coming together, can make one, or, sometimes, two—twins being the largest number she had ever been called upon to deliver. And Blister was even more ignorant than that.

Although she knew her trade in every particular, and could have delivered a baby as safely as kiss-your-hand, she'd no more idea of how the seed had been planted than she knew what happened to the River Thames after it went past Wapping. Moss had never seen fit to enlighten her. In Moss's view, all that Blister needed to know was how to get babies out; getting them in was no part of the trade. The nearest she ever came to telling Blister was at Christmastide when she went on, with a radiant smile, about a woman being with child of the Holy Ghost. This made Blister very frightened; she had nightmares of being confronted, when she least expected it, by something inexpressibly fierce in a sheet.

Presently they reached Glass House Yard, and there was Mr Greening's shop, leaking light and commotion at every joint. They began to cross the dark cobbles, when Moss cried out.

"Stop! Stop!" She halted in her tracks with her arms spread out so that her cape fell down like a pair of mildewy

GREENING
cut and Silvered

wings. Something had darkened her path.

"Black cat, Blister! Cross your fingers and think of wood—else the baby will be wrong way round!!"

Obediently Blister dropped her bag, crossed her fingers and emptied her mind of everything except a broomstick that stood behind Moss's kitchen door. It was the only wood she knew.

"Done it, mum."

Moss heaved a sigh of relief and advanced upon the premises of Mr Greening.

"You can't be too careful," she said, giving her famous double knock upon the door. "Not where such 'appiness is at stake!"

"They're 'ere! They're 'ere! Thank Gawd you've come! Mr Greening—it's the midwife! Mrs Greening! It's all right now! Oh thank Gawd you're 'ere! They're all goin' off their 'eads! Is it always like this, marm?"

Mr Greening's apprentice, who was small and sharp like a weasel, and who nursed ambitions of becoming one of the family, was quite beside himself with anxiety and excitement as he admitted Moss and Blister through the trade counter that occupied the entrance of the establishment. "They'll remember this," he thought to himself as he took Moss's cape and offered to assist Blister with her bag. "They'll remember how I give up me Christmas and worritted myself sick like a son!"

Mr Greening himself appeared. He was an ugly man with a nose like a warty old potato. He was a silverer of mirrors, which was an unusual trade for one of his unlucky appearance.

"Thank God you've come!" he cried.

Next came the Greenings' two daughters, young ladies of twelve and fourteen, and quite as ugly as their father.

"Thank God you're here! We thought ma was going to die!"

Then a maidservant looked in, and a neighbour's wife, and *they* thanked God for Moss, so that Moss felt deliciously holy all over. With a wave of her hand she dispatched Blister upstairs to see how things were proceeding; then she went into the warm bright parlour to receive whatever else of respect, gratitude and hospitality might be coming her way.

"This way, miss! Do let me carry yer bag. Gawd, it's 'eavy!" exclaimed the weaselish apprentice as he conducted Blister up the stairs and towards the room from which Mrs Greening could be heard moaning and peevishly inquiring where everyone had gone. "Wotcher got in it, miss? The Crahn jewels?"

"Instryments," said Blister. "Knives and forksips and fings."

"Gawd," said Mr Greening's apprentice. "It's a real business, ain't it?"

Blister smiled proudly and the weaselish one couldn't help reflecting that the saucer-eyed Blister was a raving beauty compared with the two Miss Greenings at whom he'd set his cap in the hopes of marrying one of them—he didn't care which—and inheriting the business.

"Make much money at it?"

"Not on Christmas Eve," said Blister. "We don't charge then."

"Why ever not?"

"Ain't you 'eard? It's on account of the Son of God might be comin'. It's all written down."

"I never 'eard of that one!"

"You're pig-ignorant, you are," said Blister, loftily.

"No more'n you. 'ow would you silver a mirror?"

"Dunno. 'ow would yer deliver a hinfant arse first?"

"Send for you! What's yer name?"

"Blister. 's on account of me skin bein' all bubbly when I come out. What's your name?"

"Bosun. It's on account of me family bein' Bosuns."

"I never 'ad a family. I was given to Moss when she

delivered me. Sort of present. Moss took a fancy to me, called me Blister and brung me up."

"Like 'er daughter?"

"'prentice. She ain't got a daughter . . ."

Bosun nodded and, with an affable smile, stood aside for Blister to enter Mrs Greening's room.

The lady lay in her bed, weeping and groaning that all the world had abandoned her, that nobody cared any more and that she was going to die.

There was indeed some reason for this latter fear as she was advanced in years and had begun to believe herself past the age of child-bearing. Like Sarah of old when the messengers from God had crossed the plain of Mamre to tell Abraham that his wife was with child, Mrs Greening had laughed when Moss had called and left her card. She'd leaned behind the door and laughed at the stout little angel of the annunciation till the tears had run down her cheeks.

But then, as the days and weeks had gone by, she'd come to laugh on the other side of her face; for Moss had been right and the mirror-maker's wife did indeed "have a little reflection in the glass".

"I'm going to die," moaned Mrs Greening, seeing that her visitor was only the midwife's gawky apprentice. "It's true—it's true!"

"Yus'm," said Blister, who had been taught there were two things in the world that there was no sense in arguing with: bad weather and a woman in labour.

She opened her bag and began to set out the instruments on a table. They were a ferocious assortment: scalpels,

cruelly curved bistouries, probes, leathern forceps, scissors and a bone-saw that, from age and infirmity, had lost all but a few of its harsh teeth. Moss had picked them up, as she liked to call it, at various stages in her career when she'd attended in the presence of surgeons. She hadn't the faintest notion what they were for; the only instruments she actually used were her small strong hands and a pair of dressmaker's scissors she'd also picked up and which she kept in her pocket to cut the umbilical cord. Nevertheless she insisted that Blister always lay out the whole surgical armoury as she felt the sight of it gave her a real professional standing and the air of one who was not to be trifled with.

Mrs Greening, watching Blister's preparations, lost her fears in a terrified awe; dying was nothing beside what her imagination had suddenly proposed. Blister, sensing the lady's respect, felt proud; but at the same time she couldn't help wishing the weaselish apprentice outside the door could also behold her in her importance.

She'd been quite taken with Bosun and had been flattered by his admiration for the mystery of her craft.

"You must keep yer mouf shut, marm," she said, loudly enough for Bosun to hear and be further impressed by her wisdom. "Breeve froo yer nose."

"Why must I do that?"

"'case yer baby's born wivout sense or soul. Gets out froo yer mouf, marm."

For the time being, Mrs Greening gave up groaning and shut her mouth.

"That's it, marm," said Blister, and went to unlatch the window. "Mustn't 'ave nuffink shut," she said. "Else yer labour will be 'ard as nails. Winders, doors, boxes, cupboards, drors . . . all got to be open. An' bockles, of course—"

"What?"

"Bockles—bockles! No stoppers or corks in 'em. Anyfink corked up corks up you, too."

"Tell Bosun," said Mrs Greening feebly.

But there was no need; Bosun had heard.

"Right away, Mrs G.! Don't you fret, marm! Bosun'll open everything!"

With a sound of thunder, Bosun was off, turning keys, lifting lids, opening bottles and dragging out crowded, obstinate drawers. "They'll remember this," he thought, "when I comes to ask for the 'and of one of them ugly girls. They'll remember 'ow Bosun ran 'is feet off like a lovin' son!"

"Knots," said Blister. "Mustn't 'ave nuffink tied nor knotted. Twists you up, else. If you got a norse or a dawg,

it's got to be untied, else the hinfant won't be able to get out."

All these strange requirements, these pebbles of magical wisdom that were laid up in Blister's head, had been gathered by Moss in her rollings among mothers and grandmothers whose memories stretched back to the beginnings of time. Moss had taken them all in, rejecting nothing, however far-fetched, and passed them on to her apprentice with the deep words: "You can't be too careful; not where such 'appiness is at stake!"

"I think it's dead!" said Mrs Greening in a sudden panic. "I can't feel it any more! It's dead—it's dead!"

"Yus'm," said Blister, and, drawing back Mrs Greening's bedclothes, bent down and laid her large, sticking-out ear to Mrs Greening's hugely swollen belly.

Now as no one was talking about Blister, her ears were as cold as ice.

"Mother of God!" shrieked Mrs Greening; and Blister started in pleased surprise to hear herself thus addressed.

"Yus'm?"

"The pain! The pain!"

Downstairs in the parlour, Moss was sipping port wine, which always imparted a rare skill to her fingers, and a brightness to her eyes.

"Never put the stopper on, sir," she said reproachfully to Mr Greening; and gently, but firmly, she took the decanter into her own hands and refilled her glass. "Nor clasp your 'ands nor cross your legs, else the baby'll never come."

Mr Greening compressed his sensible lips and cast his eyes towards the ceiling. Nevertheless, he obeyed the midwife's injunction. Even as he did so, everyone heard Mrs Greening shriek out, and directly after came Blister's shout:

"She's started! Come on up, marm! She's on the way!"

The mirror-maker stared down in bewilderment at his uncrossed knees and everyone else in the parlour looked terrified as if they'd just received an inkling of a mysterious web of laws in which they were all caught, like so many helpless flies. The neighbour's wife, who had been inclined to regard Moss's superstitions with contempt, now stared at the fat little midwife with a respect that bordered on dread. And so she should have done; for Moss knew very well what she was about, and was right to neglect nothing when such happiness was at stake.

Moss finished off her wine and rose to her feet.

"I'll call you," she said, "when it's over."

She left the parlour and briskly mounted the stairs. Outside Mrs Greening's door, she came upon Bosun who had gone very white in the face as the cries and grunts from within increased in urgency.

"You must cover up all the mirrors," she told him; "else the baby will be born blind."

Bosun nodded and prepared to fly at the midwife's bidding. She raised her hand.

"And put neither wood nor coal on the fire till the cord's cut; else the baby might be born dead."

"I never knew, I never guessed there was so much to it, marm."

"You can't be too careful," said Moss, sombrely, "where such 'appiness is at stake."

Bosun fled. "They'll remember this," he thought. "They'll remember 'ow Bosun was a real son to them!"

By the time he'd scoured the premises and covered up every last glimmer of reflecting silver and returned to his station outside the bedroom door, matters were far advanced. Panting and gulping, he listened . . .

"'old 'er legs, Blister! Up a bit . . ."

"Yus'm."

"Bear down, mother! Bear down wiv all yer might!"

"I can't! I can't!"

"'old your breff when it comes on! 'old yer breff when you feel it pushin' . . ."

"It's burning me—it's burning me like fire!"

"Bear down agin, mother! Blister! Give 'er knees another shove! Push, mother! Push like ye'r rollin' a cart of 'ay!"

"I can't . . . I—I've no more strength!"

"'old yer breff agin! Ah! I can see it! Luvly little thing! Ye'r all but crownin' now, mother!"

"No—no! I don't want to! It's going to kill me! Stop it!"

"'eave ho! 'eave ho!"

But Mrs Greening was still reluctant to bring forth the little "reflection in her glass", and she began to curse and swear in a way that made Bosun's toes curl up. He'd no idea his mistress knew such words, nor was so wild and abandoned a soul as she sounded.

"'eave ho! 'eave ho! mother," urged Moss; and there followed a most awesome grunting, as of stout hawsers straining when the full tide heaves a great vessel to tug against its moorings.

"Ugh! Ugh! Ugh!"

"'eave ho! 'eave ho!"

"Ugh! Ugh! Ugh!"

"Don't let 'er go, Blister!"

"Yus'm."

"There ain't nothing knotted anywhere, Blister?"

"Bosun!" screeched out Blister anxiously.

"Yes, miss?"

"Boot laces! Got 'em undone?"

Bosun looked down. His shoes were tightly laced—and double-knotted. Guiltily he bent down and tried to untie them. His fingers shook and trembled, but the knots defeated him. Mrs Greening moaned and groaned; Moss urged her to still greater efforts—and Bosun pulled and snapped his laces.

"Done it—done it, miss!" he shouted in triumph; and Mrs Greening gave a last mighty cry.

"Clever girl!" said Moss. "Blister! Get me scissors out, there's a dear!"

"Yus'm."

"Look what a luvly little thing it is! All its fingers and toes! Listen—listen! Ah! There it goes!"

Suddenly there came a fragile sound, so thin and winding that it scarcely seemed to make its way through the air. It was the sound of a voice, brand new, never before heard since the beginning of time.

"And I done it!" thought Bosun, looking down incredulously at his broken boot laces. "Oh, they'll remember this when I comes to offer meself as their son!"

"Tell Mr Greening!" sighed the mother's exhausted, happy voice. "I want Mr Greening to come . . ."

"Bosun!"

"Yes, miss?"

"Go tell 'em it's over and everyfing's all right! Tell Mr Greenin' to come on up an' 'ave a look at 'is wife an' son!"

"They'll remember this," thought Bosun, flying down the stairs, "when I'm their SON!"

The last word came out aloud, in a dismayed grunt and squeal. A son! But now they'd already got one!

In the twinkling of an eye the apprentice's ambitions tumbled as the tiny creature he himself had done so much to deliver safely, usurped his prospects. He saw it all. It would grow and grow and, sooner or later, come to lord it over him; Bosun would count for nothing; the newcomer would inherit the business . . .

"You got a son, Mr Greening," he said, entering the expectant parlour and doing his best to keep the dismay out of his voice. "You got a bruvver," he said, gazing mournfully at the two ugly daughters. At least, he thought, he would no longer have to worry which of them would be the least disagreeable to marry. It's an ill wind, he reflected wryly, that don't blow at least *some* good!

Everyone in the parlour exclaimed aloud with joy and began hastening upstairs; while Bosun—passed-over Bosun—went about fastening latches, closing doors and corking up all the bottles with the vague, melancholy feeling that he was bolting the stable door after the horse had gone. He looked down at his loosened shoes. He sighed.

"And I'll even 'ave to buy meself new laces!"

He peered into the fire he'd just replenished and tried to see castles in the coals. "They've forgotten," he thought; "they've forgotten all about Bosun now." He shifted a piece of coal to make a roof for what would have been a fine mansion; but it fell through and the walls collapsed into blazing ruins. "'ow like life," whispered Bosun. "'ow like life!"

"Bosun?"

"Yes, miss?"

Blister had come down; she looked flushed and disarranged from her recent efforts. Even her ears stuck out more than usual; like a pair of cupboard doors, thought Bosun, bitterly. He couldn't help regarding her as the part author of his misfortune.

"Mr Greenin' says you're to gimme a glass of port wine to drink 'is son's elf."

"Yes, miss."

"An' 'e says you're to 'ave one yerself."

"I ain't thirsty," said Bosun; but nevertheless he joined Blister. There was, after all, no law that could make him drink to the infant who had just done him out of his inheritance.

"'ere's to seein' your face in the glass!" he said, defiantly.

"'ere's to the Son of God!"

"The son of Greening, you mean."

Blister shook her head wisely.

"It's got to come in a stable, wiv' free kings an' a donkey and a special star."

"That'll be the day!"

"It'll come; one Christmas Eve. It's all written down."

"And will you be there to 'elp?"

"I'll be there," said Blister, shutting her saucer eyes tightly and swilling down her wine. "Me an' the 'oly Ghost."

She swallowed and opened her eyes, and the two apprentices gazed at one another over the tops of their glasses: the one mournful, the other still full of hope. In one, ambition had fallen; in the other, it still remained in the skies.

"She ain't really such a bad looker," thought Bosun. "In a narrer glass you'd never see them ears!"

"'ave another glass of wine!" offered Bosun, feeling distinctly less careful over his master's property than he would have done, half an hour before.

"Yus!" said Blister, thrusting out her long, thin arm.

Bosun recharged the glasses and smiled somewhat crookedly.

"'ere's to seein' *your* face in the glass!" said Blister, politely echoing her companion's toast.

"And 'ere's to the Son of God!" responded Bosun. They drank.

"'ave"—began Bosun, when there came a loud knocking on the street door. Bosun frowned and put down his glass.

"'elp yourself," he said; and then added broodingly, "we all got to 'elp ourselves, miss."

He left the parlour and clattered through the shop. Blister felt a gust of cold night air come sweeping in as the street door was opened; she shivered. Bosun returned.

"It's for you. Midwife wanted. In a 'urry. 'ow did they know you was 'ere?"

"We allus tell a neighbour in Glastonbury Court. They 'ave to know where to find us. Moss!" screeched Blister.

"What is it, Blister?"

"Anuvver call! In a 'urry!"

"Whereabouts?"

Blister looked inquiringly at Bosun.

"Said it were in Three Kings Court."

"Free Kings Court, Moss!"

"*Three Kings?*" Moss's voice took on an edge of excitement. "What 'ouse?"

"New Star public 'ouse," said Bosun.

"The Noo Star, Moss!" howled Blister.

"The Star? The New Star?" repeated Moss, from upstairs. "Christmas Eve, three kings and a new star? Blister! Come an' fetch yer instryments! Blister! It might be the one! 'urry, girl, 'urry!"

Blister and Bosun stared at one another. Curiosity and excitement filled the heart of one apprentice; apprehension and dread clutched at the other.

Could it really be the one? thought Blister. Never! Three kings and an inn called the New Star weren't enough. It had to be more than that. Partly relieved, she ran upstairs to collect her instruments.

"Carry yer bag, miss?" offered Bosun impulsively, as Blister came down again in the wake of the fat and trembling Moss.

"Wot? All the way to Free Kings Court? Won't they miss you 'ere?"

"Not now they got a son," said Bosun, bitterly. "Besides," he went on, brightening a little, "if it's *im*'—you know, the one what we drunk to—I'd like to see 'im. Wouldn't want to miss 'im. It'd be summat to remember all right."

"It won't be 'im," said Blister, thrusting out her lower lip. "It can't be 'im. It needs more'n free kings and a star . . ."

"'urry, Blister! 'urry!" Moss was already in the street. "What if it's reely 'im an' we're too late?"

There they went, Moss and Blister, hurrying by starlight, with Bosun clanking the bag of instruments and keeping a watch for footpads and other demons of the night. They hastened up Water Street and into Ludgate Hill . . .

"It's got to be in a stable!" panted Blister.

"'appy Christmas, 'appy Christmas!" called out a pair of watchmen on Fleet Bridge who were warming themselves before a brazier of glowing coals that threw up their faces in a ruddy comfort amid the empty fields of the night.

"Look, Blister, girl! Shepherds abidin' . . . and the glory of the Lord shinin' all round 'em! Make 'aste, make 'aste! I reely think it might be the night!"

But it took more than that to convince Blister. She shook her head so violently that tiny drops of salt water flew out of her saucer eyes.

"It ain't the night! It ain't!" she muttered, as they passed Temple Bar and came into the Strand. "There's got to be frankincense and—and more!"

"What's frankincense?" asked Bosun, ready to come upon it at any moment if only he knew what to look for.

Blister did not answer; she was in no mood to tempt fate. Moss put on a spurt of speed and scuttled on ahead. Still shaking her head, Blister stalked after, into Southampton Street and Covent Garden. Bosun, burdened with the heavy bag, came panting up beside her.

"And—and there's got to be a donkey," mumbled Blister, putting yet another obstacle in the way of Moss's heart's desire, "and a wise man from the east."

As they drew near Three Kings Court, her great saucers were awash with new tears. She bit her lip and clenched her fists; and then, wickedness of wickedness, she secretly knotted a corner of her cape and vowed to keep her fingers crossed against the coming, that night, of the Son of God. It had to be her, and her alone, who was to be got with child of the Holy Ghost. She peered furtively up to the stars.

"'ere I am," she whimpered. "Blister! It's me you're lookin' for! Me! Down 'ere. Me wiv the big ears . . ."

Thus Blister, in her bottomless ignorance, strove with all her might and main to prevent the second coming on that Christmas Eve. That such an event would mark the end of the world's misery meant nothing to Blister. What would be the good of it? In the middle of all the happiness she would have remained the one black spot of woe; and made all the darker by the thoughtless brightness all around. Moss would forget her in the excitement; Moss would be on her knees before a stranger, and Blister would be out in the cold . . .

At last they came to Three Kings Court where a single lantern lit up the frontage of the New Star Inn. Despite its name, the New Star was the oldest building in the court. It was left over from the days when Covent Garden had been a convent garden and had supplied the palace of Westminster with fruit and vegetables. Since then, however, tall tenements had come crowding in, imprisoning the New Star and taking away its pleasant garden. Only the coaching yard remained to mark its former glory; but even that was a mockery as no vehicle could possibly have gained entry to the court through the narrow passage that was all that the greedy builders had seen fit to leave as a way in.

There was, in point of fact, a bulky, old-fashioned coach still standing in a corner of the cobbled yard. It was a dreamy, melancholy sight that suggested a great journey abandoned, or a faithful love discarded and forgotten in the haste of new prospects. For a time it had been used as a trysting place; but when the roof had rotted and the seats decayed, it had become a playground for children . . .

Under the arch that formed the entrance to the yard stood a grimy, oil-smelling lamplighter who lived nearby. It was he who was holding the lantern and swinging it, turning the night into an earthquake of sliding shadows.

"She's in there," he said to Moss.

"Where?"

"In the stable."

Moss turned to Blister and Bosun. Her face was ecstatic.

"It's no good!" whispered Blister. "There's got to be a donkey, too!"

They passed under the arch and crossed the yard. The lamplighter followed them, and his swaying lantern was reflected in the windows of the derelict coach so that it

seemed, for a moment, that the abandoned vehicle had come to life and was inhabited by a procession of spirits bearing candles . . .

The inn-keeper's wife, hearing the footsteps on the cobbles, hastened out to meet the midwife.

"We wouldn't have known a thing about it," she explained. "She came in so quiet. It was only on account of her beast braying out that gave her away. And then we came out and found her . . ."

"Her beast?"

"She came on a donkey. It's in the stable now, eating its head off—"

"A donkey? A donkey! Gawd! Did you 'ear that, Blister?"

Blister heard. "There's got to be a wise man," she moaned softly.

"She's some sort of gipsy," went on the inn-keeper's wife. "She's as dark as a nut. Come up from Kent, we fancy, selling apples. They thieve 'em out of barns down there, and travel into London on their donkeys like regular apple-sellers. She must have been took short in the Strand. She was squatting in the old coach when we found her. At first we thought she was just poorly . . . so we took her into the stable as we'd got no rooms in the house it the moment. Then we saw what it was. She's very near her time . . ."

Although the inn-keeper's wife tried to be casual and off-hand in her account, it was plain that she, no less than Moss, was moved by the strange and prophetic nature of the circumstance. Perhaps all this had been in her mind when she and her husband had decided to move the gipsy into the stable? Perhaps this is the way prophecies are meant to be fulfilled? *Seek, and ye shall find; knock, and it shall be opened unto you.*

Two lamps, that had once lit the ancient coach on its way, shed their light now over the stall where the gipsy had found refuge in her distress, and a bucket of burning coals had been placed in a swept corner to give some warmth in the freezing night. The sight thus illumined was old and strange, full of mysterious shadows and still more mysterious light. There was the donkey, half emerging from the gloom and bowing its gentle head to nibble at the straw on which its mistress lay. Further back, half hidden

by the wooden partition, stood the inn-keeper and t
three travellers who had been putting up for the night
dim light rendered their faces intent and profound . .

"We've not managed to get a word out of her," con
the inn-keeper's wife; "that we can understand, th
She gabbled away in her own lingo when we took he
of the coach; but as soon as she saw we meant her no h
she buttoned up her lip and she's been quiet as a m
ever since."

The gipsy was dark, brown as a nut. Her hair was b
and was braided cunningly over her ears so that her oval face seemed to have been laid in a basket of black straw. Her eyes were as black as her hair and fixed themselves on Moss with a look that was at once suspicious and defiant. Only the drops of sweat that stood upon her high forehead betrayed that she was in any difficulty or pain.

"It's very unusual," murmured one of the travellers, "for any of her race to be abandoned at such a time. She must be an outcast of some description . . ."

"This gentleman seems to know a thing or two," said the inn-keeper's wife softly. "He's what you might call a wise man." As she said this, she gave a curious smile and a little nod to Moss. Blister wept; she stood alone before the inexorable power of fate.

Moss, her joints crackling like gunfire, knelt down beside the gipsy. Reverently she laid a hand, first on the woman's brow and then on her rusty black gown through which she strove to feel the motions of the child within. She looked up at Blister and nodded. Dully, Blister took her bag from Bosun and began to lay out her instruments on the straw.

The gipsy watched the preparations impassively, and then transferred her gaze to Blister herself. Hastily Blister looked away. She dreaded that the woman, full of the mysterious gifts of her race, would be able to spy out the devil of jealousy that dwelt in Blister's soul.

The gipsy frowned, and bit on her red, red lip. Moss, observing this, drew in her breath sharply.

"Go see nothing's locked nor tied nor stopped up," she murmured to Blister. "I think 'e's comin' and we must make 'is way straight, like it says."

Blister swallowed and retreated from the stall.

"I'll 'elp!" offered Bosun excitedly. He attempted to press Blister's hand under cover of darkness, but Blister shrank away . . .

"The donkey!" burst out Bosun, coming up upon Blister

suddenly. "You forgot it! But no matter—I untied 'im!"

Blister stared at the weaselish apprentice with misery. He departed.

"There was a bit of old 'arness," he said, appearing beside Blister again, "'angin' on a 'ook. I unbuckled it!"

Blister clenched her fists and the weasel scuttled busily off.

"There was an ol' bottle in the corner . . . I took the cork out! Don't you worrit, miss! I'll do what's needful . . . for the sake of '*im*!!"

Blister moaned.

"There was a copper pan polished so's you could see yer face in it. But I covered it up!"

Blister snarled, and Bosun, mistaking the sound for anxiety, reached out to comfort Blister.

"Miss—miss! There's a knot got into yer cape! 'old still and I'll undo it. There—"

Helplessly Blister submitted; she dared not let it be known what was in her heart.

"Blister! Come quick!"

Moss's voice was summoning her. She stared wildly towards the stall. The inn-keeper and the travellers had moved back, out of decency and respect. A glow seemed to rise up from where the gipsy lay. Suddenly this glow became fiercely bright!

"I just put a bit of wood on the fire," murmured the inn-keeper's wife; "to keep her warm."

"Never do that!" squealed Bosun. "That were wrong!" He rushed inside the stall and, burning his fingers, snatched the brand from the burning bucket and doused it in a barrel of water that stood nearby.

He smiled at Blister as she entered the stall.

"I 'opes," he said, sucking his injured fingers, "that *'e* remembers this when we all come to be judged."

Thereupon Bosun retired to the darkest part of the stable, where, with the inn-keeper and the travellers, he awaited the birth of the saviour.

"Blister!"

"Yus'm?"

"Down 'ere! What the matter wiv you, girl? 'old the lady's knees. Gently—gently, girl! Remember what she

might be! Oh my Gawd! She's all but crownin' and not a word nor a cry! It's a mirricle, all right!"

Blister, leaning forward and pressing on the gipsy's bent knees, put her face close and breathed fiercely:

"Were it the 'oly Ghost? Tell us—tell us!"

The gipsy's dark eyes widened and swam with moisture.

"Blister!"

"Yus'm?"

"What are you on at? Don't fret 'er! It's comin'! I—I can see 'is 'ead! It's 'im all right! It must be! 'e's *shinin'*!"

Bosun, in the shadows, heard the midwife's rapturous cry. The coming of the saviour instantly produced in his mind thoughts of a world where apprentices were level with their masters, where there was no toil to blunt the nights and days.

Moss thought of herself in a stained-glass window, offering the Son of God to the black-haired Queen of Heaven; while Blister, her apprentice, saw herself cast into the outer darkness, despised and rejected alike of the Holy Ghost and Moss and all mankind.

She glared, with fearful desperation, into the gipsy's eyes. She pretended to yawn, stretching wide her mouth. The gipsy looked suddenly frightened; she tried to clench her teeth against the awful power of Blister's example. An expression of terrified pleading came into her eyes as she strained. Blister was the devil, encouraging her to lose her child's soul through her open mouth! A great shudder convulsed her and she shook her head from side to side.

"Blister—Blister, my love!" sobbed Moss. "That it should be us . . . together . . . on this night! Oh Blister, I knew, when I 'eld you in me arms, that you and me would do summat wonderful! Oh Blister! That were a blessed night when you was born!"

As she heard these words, Blister's heart lifted up. It had been a blessed night when she'd been born! She shut her mouth, and the gipsy bestowed on her a smile of the most wondrous radiance.

"Scissors, Blister! Where's me scissors? Quick, girl! What are you at?"

Bosun, staring towards the stall, believed he saw a radiance rising up as the glorious new life began. Then came the cry, like a thread of gold . . . Everyone pressed forward eagerly.

"Oh Blister!" cried Moss, her voice shaking. "Oh Blister! We wasn't worthy after all! It—it ain't 'im! It—it's a girl!"

Hopes raised foolishly, settled into ashes. The travellers went back to their rooms and the gipsy nursed her child while her donkey nodded and nibbled. The inn-keeper's wife, rueful of countenance, bade the midwife farewell, and the old coach in the yard looked deader than ever as Moss, Blister and Bosun passed it by.

"If only," said Bosun to Blister, "they'd been the other way round. If only there'd been a girl at Mr Greening's and a boy 'ere! What a night that would 'ave been, eh?"

He sighed and pondered on how nearly he and the world had come to being saved.

"If only it 'ad been a boy!" sighed Moss, sniffing and

dabbing her eyes.

"We'd never 'ave 'ad to work again," said Bosun.

"There'd be no more dyin'," said Moss.

"There'd be no more rainin' on Sundays," said Bosun.

"There'd be no more damp winters," said Moss. "And no more growin' old."

"There'd be strawberries all the year round," said Bosun; "growin' in the streets."

"We'd all be wed," said Moss; "wiv never a death to part us."

"We'd all be beautiful," said weaselish Bosun. "There wouldn't be a ugly face anywhere."

He glanced at Blister, who was gazing up to the stars. Blister alone was neither mournful nor full of regrets. She was smiling, a strange, secret smile. She had not been rejected, either of the Holy Ghost, or Moss, or mankind. She *had* been visited; she knew it. She smiled and smiled at the stars. Bosun continued to watch her and found her mysterious and quite heart-catching. Blister, feeling his scrutiny, looked into his eyes.

"All we needed was a boy," sighed Moss.

"All we needed was a boy," repeated Blister; and the two apprentices—the one like a beanpole, the other like a weasel—continued to gaze into each other's eyes.

"'appy Christmas!" called the lamplighter, who still stood under the archway that led out into Three Kings Court. "*For unto us a Son is born!*"

"It were a girl," said Moss sadly. "We needed a boy."

"But I got a boy," murmured Blister.

"You got a boy," agreed Bosun, and took her by the hand.

There they go, Moss, Blister and Bosun, hurrying through the dark streets.

"Moss!" called out Blister. "It were '*im*, after all."

Moss turned and looked back at Blister and then at Bosun. She smiled and nodded.

"In a manner o' speakin', dear," she said. "In a manner o' speakin'."